The Legend of
The Painted Turtle

Written by Blake Maher
Illustrated by Joshua Maher

First Printing, 2014

ISBN: 978-0-692-28550-3

Cousin Small Books, 2517 2nd Street B, Santa Monica, CA 90405
www.CousinSmallBooks.com

To the children of The Painted Turtle,
with thanks for the color with
which they paint the world.

Once upon a time,
a long, long time ago,
when the world
was very young ...

... there was
a turtle who
wandered all
the time in search
of a home.

He was not the kind
of turtle that we think
about today with
a hard, tough shell
to protect him,

but instead he
was the kind of
turtle we might find if
we slid a turtle right out
of his shell—one with
a skinny green body, soft
and tender, with little to
protect him from the harsh
elements of the world.

For many, many
years the turtle had
been searching for
a safe place to live
and call home.

Because without any
protection he was always
afraid of the other animals
that might have a taste
for a good turtle soup.

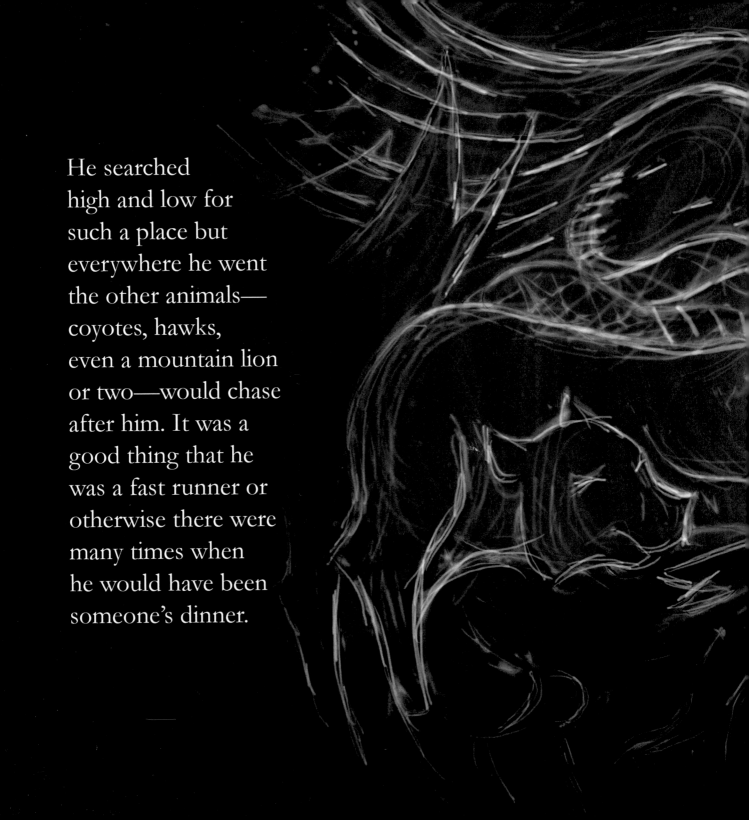

He searched
high and low for
such a place but
everywhere he went
the other animals—
coyotes, hawks,
even a mountain lion
or two—would chase
after him. It was a
good thing that he
was a fast runner or
otherwise there were
many times when
he would have been
someone's dinner.

Finally one day the
turtle found himself
wandering through
the high desert.

It was hot and dry,
and the big vast sky
and scarce trees left
him feeling exposed
and unprotected
from his enemies.

But the turtle made
it through the first few
days and gradually he
began to make friends
with a few of the other
creatures in the area,
with the lizards,
the rabbits, a bird
here and there.

He even sang a few times
with the field mice who
liked to sing at the moon,
although in general
he thought the mice
to be a bit silly.

One day when a particularly
nasty hawk kept swooping
down on the turtle,
trying to snap him up
in its beak, a rabbit signaled
to the turtle from her hole
and helped him hide inside
until the hawk got tired
and flew away.

The turtle thought to himself,
"Well, this is a fine how-do-you-do.
Who would have thought a
rabbit could protect me?"

For the very first time
it occurred to him that
one of the forms of
protection he always
had with him was
his friends.

He gathered together
this idea of friendship
and stuck it on his back
where it made a round
shape and took on
the bluish color
of an early night sky.

After a few days it
grew hard and solid on
his back and to his surprise
he realized that when other
animals tried to attack him now
he could always count on this
piece of friendship to protect him.

Another night,
the turtle was
out strolling
in the moonlight
when a coyote
began to howl
at him in a very
hungry way.

A group of field mice singing at the moon
motioned for him to take cover in an old
hollow log nearby. At first the turtle was
nervous about trusting the mice—
"field mice can sing like the dickens
but they're as silly as can be,"
he thought to himself.

But the mice said,
"We're here to help you, turtle,"
and so the turtle trusted them
and hid inside the log.
After a while the coyote
grew tired of circling the log
and left the turtle alone.

The turtle was glad he
had trusted the field
mice and began
to understand that
trusting in the
right friends was
something that
could help in
difficult times too.
So the turtle shaped
his trust together
in a solid plate
and put it on
his back.

Soon afterward it too
had hardened beside
the blue piece
of friendship,
only this time it
was as tough as
a stone and
as red as
a heart.

The turtle soon
began to find that
the same thing
happened with
kindness and courage
and laughter and love.
Every time he took
one of these gifts from
his friends and stored
them on his back
they served to protect
him, each taking on
a different color of
yellow or orange or
purple or green.

In no time at all the
turtle had a marvelous
many-colored shell that
he wore on his back
as the best kind of
protection in life,
that of friends who
cared about him.

And soon
those animals that
had once hunted him
found that if they chased
after the turtle now he simply
pulled into his shell—
his home—created by
the love of all those
around him.

It's true he wasn't quite
as fast a runner anymore,
but who cared
about speed when
you had love?

Today the painted turtle lives for many, many years. And why is that you might ask?

Well, it's because the turtle learned
that the protection we need in life
is found in those around us, from
kindness and friendship, from respect
and trust. These are the things that
are important in life. These are the
things that help us to endure.

So take a lesson from the turtle
and gather around you that which
is important. If you do this, you'll
never be far from your home.

ACKNOWLEDGMENTS

Special thanks to Bill Villafranco and the
Virginia B. Toulmin Foundation whose
generosity has made this book possible.

Thank you to the children and summer
staff members of The Painted Turtle
who have helped bring this tale to life.

A portion of the proceeds from the
sale of *The Legend of the Painted Turtle* will
support The Painted Turtle, a SeriousFun
Camp founded by Paul Newman for
children with chronic and life-threatening
medical conditions. To learn more, visit
www.thepaintedturtle.org.

Blake Maher is the Executive Director of The Painted Turtle, a SeriousFun Camp founded by Paul Newman for children with serious medical conditions. He has helped lead camp-based programs for children in both the United States and abroad.

He wrote *The Legend of The Painted Turtle* before the camp opened in the hope of what the camp might someday offer to the children who came through its gates. His writing has been published in magazines and newspapers across the country. He lives in Santa Monica, California.

Joshua Maher is an artist and graphic designer. He worked at The Painted Turtle as the Arts and Crafts Lead for two of the best summers of his life. The spirit and bravery of the campers he met there served as his inspiration for these illustrations. He lives with his family in Massachusetts.

18325303R00023